20,000 L
Under th

by
Jules Verne

adapted by
Malvina G. Vogel

Illustrations by
Pablo Marcos Studio

MOBY BOOKS

Published by Playmore Inc., Publishers,
230 Fifth Avenue, New York, N.Y. 10001
and Waldman Publishing Corp.,
570 Seventh Avenue, New York, N.Y. 10018

Copyright © MCMLXXVII by
Playmore Inc., Publishers and Waldman Publishing Corp.,
New York, New York

 **MOBY BOOKS is a registered trademark
of Waldman Publishing Corp., New York, New York**

Printed in Canada

CONTENTS

About the Author

Jules Verne was born in 1828 in the seaport town of Nantes, France. As a boy, Jules sat at the docks listening to sailors' tales of faraway places and imagining himself exploring unknown worlds. But when he attempted a seagoing adventure himself, his father pulled twelve-year-old Jules off a ship bound for India. A severe beating led Jules to promise, "From now on, I'll travel only in my imagination."

And travel he did! In over one hundred books and stories, Jules Verne took his readers on imaginary journeys inside volcanoes, under oceans, over unexplored countries, to the moon, and around distant planets.

His heroes traveled in balloons, steam tanks, rocket ships, submarines, electric autos, and mechanically-driven islands.

These inventions may not seem surprising today, but Jules Verne predicted these wonders over one hundred years ago, when men traveled by horse and carriage and when steam engines were just being developed. Yet Verne made all his inventions believable because he explained them with accurate scientific details.

Thirty years before an actual ocean-going submarine was developed, Verne's remarkable *Nautilus* was sailing *20,000 Leagues Under the Sea*.

When Jules Verne died in 1905, many of the inventions he had predicted had already become realities. But Verne would have been pleased to know that the U.S. Navy was so inspired by his underwater invention, that it named its first atomic submarine—the *U.S.S. Nautilus*—in honor of the man who many said "invented the future."

The Mysterious "Thing"

Chapter 1
The Mysterious Monster

The year 1866 was marked by several strange and mysterious events at sea. Ships from many countries had met an "enormous black thing" hundreds of feet long. It was larger than any creature known to scientists. The "thing" gave off an eerie glow underwater and spurted columns of water hundreds of feet into the air.

The "thing" was sighted in July off the coast of Australia, then, three days later, in the waters of the Pacific Ocean more than 2,100 miles away. The next sighting, two weeks later, was in the middle of the Atlanti Ocean, 6,000 miles away. What an extraordi nary creature this must be to move from on place to another in such a short time!

Reports of this "thing" caused great ex citement in every country of the world. Wild stories about all kinds of sea monsters ap peared in newspapers in every language o the globe. Scientists argued among them selves as to whether such a huge, speedy sea monster could exist.

Then, early in 1867, this sea monster stopped being a scientific problem and became a real danger. Merchant steamers and passengers ships were being struck by something! Was it a rock? A reef? Or this sea monster?

One ship, the *Scotia,* was examined in drydock after a collision at sea. Her engineers couldn't believe their eyes! A hole in the shape of a perfect triangle had opened up

Newspaper Stories Around the World

her thick steel hull!

I had read about these events during my visit to the United States where I was gathering plants, animals and minerals for the Paris Museum. As Professor of Natural History at the museum and as author of a book called *Mysteries of the Ocean Depths,* I Monsieur Pierre Aronnax, am considered an expert on undersea life.

But I was as puzzled about this monster as everyone else. I searched my mind for a creature that might fit the descriptions given by various sea captains. I came up with the *narwhal*—a kind of whale which can grow to a length of sixty feet. A gigantic one, hundreds of feet long, might very well exist in the unexplored ocean depths! Then too, the narwhal has a tusk as hard as steel. It could have made the hole in the hull of the *Scotia*.

The United States government decided to take steps to rid the seas of this terrible

The Narwhal

monster. A very fast warship was outfitted
with every known weapon—from harpoons to
cannons—to track down and kill the creature.

Through the kindness of President Andrew
Johnson, I was invited to join this expedition
in search of the narwhal. Together with my
loyal servant, Conseil, who for ten years had
never left my side anywhere in the world, I
boarded the warship *Abraham Lincoln*.

Commander Farragut welcomed us aboard,
and soon the ship moved out into New York
Harbor. Hundreds of ferryboats filled with
cheering people followed us for an hour. The
Abraham Lincoln lowered and raised her
thirty-nine-star American flag in thanks.

We followed the coast of Long Island east-
ward and, by nightfall, we entered the dark
waters of the Atlantic Ocean.

Boarding the *Abraham Lincoln*

Ned Land, King of Harpooners

Chapter 2
The Hunt Begins

Commander Farragut had no doubt that he would find and destroy the narwhal. After all, he had the fastest, best-armed ship in the U.S. Navy. He had a loyal, enthusiastic crew. But he had something even better—he had Ned Land, the king of Canadian harpooners!

Ned's skill and courage made him the most valuable man on board. His eyes were like a powerful telescope, sighting things at great distances. And his arm was like a mighty cannon, always ready to explode!

By the time we had been at sea three

weeks, Ned and I had become good friends
We spent hours talking about his whaling
adventures, but Ned stubbornly refused to
discuss the giant narwhal. He did not believe
it really existed.

"Why can't you accept the idea of a huge
narwhal?" I asked. "After all, you're one man
who knows all about large sea animals!"

"It's all right for ordinary people to believe
in such a creature, Professor," he replied.
"But I've hunted and harpooned hundreds of
whales. And no matter how powerful they
were, neither their tails nor their tusks were
strong enough to crack open the steel hull of
a ship. A wooden hull, yes. But never steel!"

"But suppose this creature lives several
miles deep in the ocean," I argued. "Just
think of the heavy pressure of the water
there! This creature would have to have un-
usually powerful bones to stand that pressure. A man like you, for example, at a depth

Professor Aronnax Describes the Narwhal.

of six miles, would be flattened out by that pressure. You'd look like a steam roller had run you over!"

"Good Lord!" exclaimed Ned. "Then the creature would have to be built with steel plates eight inches thick! And that's even thicker than the hull of a warship... But I still don't believe this creature exists!"

"Then how do you explain, you stubborn harpooner, what happened to the *Scotia?*"

Ned hesitated, then said, "Maybe it was a... No, no! It can't be!" And the stubborn harpooner refused to say another word.

As the *Abraham Lincoln* rounded the tip of South America and moved from the Atlantic Ocean into the Pacific, everyone began to search the surface of the ocean. Night and day, eyes and telescopes did not rest. We gulped down our meals and slept only a few hours at night.

Ned Land was the only one who refused to

Searching for the Narwhal

search the ocean, except when it was his tur
to stand watch.

"It's all nonsense!" he protested when
scolded him for his lack of interest. "Why
we're just wandering around blindly. You sa
this creature was last seen in the middle c
the Pacific. But that was four or five month
ago! If this creature travels as fast as you sa
it does, it's probably far away by now. . .if i
even exists!"

I had no answer for Ned. Yes, we wer
wandering around blindly, but what els
could we do? We had spent three month
cruising in the North Pacific, chasing whale:
and sighting reefs. We covered every mile o
ocean between the coasts of Japan and Nortl
America. But we found nothing!

Everyone on board grew discouraged, ther
angry. How could they have been foolish
enough to believe in such a ridiculous expedition? It was time to give up and return home!

Ned Isn't Interested.

But Commander Farragut persuaded his me
to wait three more days. If, during that time
the monster didn't appear, he would turn th
ship around and go back.

This promise was made on November 2
For the next three days the crew worked
harder than ever. But on November 5, when
the three days had ended with no monster
sighted, the Commander kept his promise.

That evening, we were about two hundred
miles from the coast of Japan. Conseil and I
were on deck staring out at the sea. The
crew, high up in the rigging, were still examining the horizon.

Suddenly, we heard Ned Land's voice
shouting, "Ahoy! There it is!"

Ned was pointing to a glowing oval-shaped
object beneath the sea. The glow was so
bright, even from four hundred yards away,
that my eyes hurt just looking at it. Could
this creature be charged with electricity?

"Ahoy! There It Is!"

Like an electric eel, perhaps?

"Look, look!" I cried. "It's moving. It's goin
backward. No, now forward! It's headin
right for us!"

Commander Farragut reversed the engine:
and the *Abraham Lincoln* started movin;
away from the light. Or rather, it *tried* t
move away. The strange glowing anima
rushed towards our starboard side with ter
rifying speed. But when it was twenty fee
from our hull, it stopped suddenly. Its ligh
went out and it disappeared.

In a few seconds we heard Ned cry out
"There it is, coming up on the port side!"

Ned was right! A shiny black body, shaped
like a fish, was sticking out above the water.
It had to be at least two hundred fifty feet
long! And its tail was moving so violently, it
turned the sea into foam.

Our cannons began firing and the shells
struck the black body. But instead of exploding,

The Monster Attacks.

they simply bounced off the creature's back and splashed into the water.

Just then, I leaned over the rail and saw Ned below me. He was hanging onto a pole with one hand and raising his terrible harpoon with the other. The creature was now only twenty feet away.

Suddenly, Ned's arm snapped forward. The harpoon sailed through the air. I heard a ringing noise as it seemed to hit something hard.

Two huge gushes of water shot up from the monster and washed over the deck of the ship. Then there was a horrible crash! I didn't even have time to grab onto anything before I felt myself being thrown over the railing and into the sea!

A Horrible Crash!

Conseil Rescues Professor Aronnax.

Chapter 3
An Iron Prison

I had plunged twenty feet into the sea when suddenly a powerful hand grabbed my clothes and pulled me to the surface. Then these calm words reached my ears: "If Monsieur would lean on my shoulder, Monsieur would be able to swim more easily."

I seized the arm of my faithful Conseil and gasped, "Did the crash throw you into the water too?"

"Not at all, Monsieur! It is my duty to serve you, so I jumped in after you."

"But where is our ship?" I asked.

Conseil pointed to the fading lights of the ship, now miles away. "She is badly damaged, Monsieur. And I fear that no one on board has noticed our disappearance."

Conseil kept me afloat while we shouted at the ship in the distance. But after four hours, I realized he was growing weak.

"Let me go, Conseil!" I cried.

"Never, Monsieur!" he gasped. "I would rather drown first."

By now, my hands were numb from the cold, my legs were stiff and cramped, and my mouth was filling with salt water. I let go of Conseil and lifted my head one last time. Then I began to sink. . . .

The last thing I remember was something hard knocking against me. Then I passed out.

When I opened my eyes, I was out of the water. Conseil was kneeling over me, and behind him stood Ned Land.

"Where am I?" I gasped.

The Men Grow Weak.

"On my floating island," said Ned. "I found it when I was thrown into the sea."

"A floating island?" I cried.

"You may call it that, Professor," explained Ned with a smile, "or you may call it the back of your giant narwhal. But this narwhal is bolted together with steel plates!"

I sat up and looked around. I was on top of a creature which was partly in the water and partly out. My hand pressed its skin. It was not the soft flesh which usually covers marine animals. It wasn't even the bony shell found on turtles or alligators. This skin was smooth, polished black steel! This was not a living creature! This was an underwater boat built in the shape of a fish!

I was overjoyed! A boat meant a crew, and a crew meant people!

"We've been saved!" I cried.

"Not if this boat decides to dive before its crew discovers we're here," said Ned.

A Narwhal with Steel Plates?

We had to find some opening or hatch to contact the people inside. I checked every inch of the deck, but all the steel plates seemed to be bolted together.

Ned began stamping on the steel plates and shouting at the top of his lungs, "Open up down there! Open up!"

Suddenly a loud clanking noise came from inside the boat. One of the steel plates lifted up and two men appeared at a hatch.

They wore otter-skin caps, sealskin boots, and loose-hanging clothes made of some strange material I had never seen before.

One of the men was short, with broad shoulders, strong arms, a large head, and thick black hair.

But it was the other man who interested me even more. He was rather tall, with a straight nose, firm mouth, and piercing eyes. He had the look of a calm, courageous man—a man accustomed to taking charge.

A Hatch Opens.

He was obviously the captain of this under-water boat.

The captain studied us carefully for several minutes without saying a word. Then he turned to his companion and said something in a language which I did not recognize.

Hoping that perhaps the captain understood French, I began explaining to him who we were and how we came to be on his boat.

He listened politely and quietly, but nothing on his face showed that he had understood anything I had said.

"All right, Ned, it's your turn," I said. "Try out your best English and see if you have any better luck than I did."

So Ned began the story, giving the same details I did. But he had no better luck at making himself understood than I had.

Then Conseil offered to try it in German. In his calm, soft voice, he repeated our story for the third time. But his German had the same

The Professor Tells His Story.

result as Ned's English and my French.

What language would these strangers understand? I tried once more, this time using some of the Latin I remembered from school. Still no response from the two men!

After several minutes of silence, the captain called down the hatch in his strange language. Immediately, eight crewmen came running up on deck. They grabbed us, pushed us towards the hatch, and led us down an iron ladder into total darkness.

We groped our way along a narrow gangway until we came to an opening. We were pushed through this opening, then a door was slammed shut behind us and a bolt fastened. We felt our way around iron walls, but there was no sign of windows or even of the door through which we had entered. In the darkness, we tripped over a wooden table and four stools in the center of the room.

"This is a disgrace!" shouted Ned. "We

The Prisoners Are Taken Below.

were friendly and talked to those idiots in French, English, German and Latin. Not only didn't they answer us, but they locked us in this dark iron prison as well!"

"Calm down, Ned," I said. "Anger won't get us any answers. Perhaps they. . ."

But before I could finish, the lights went on. Strange glowing lights! Then the door opened and a steward appeared. He brought us underwear, shirts, and pants—all made of that same cloth the other men wore. As we got out of our wet clothes and into dry ones, the steward began setting the table with the finest china and silver I had ever seen. Each piece had a large *N* engraved on it. Was this, perhaps, the captain's initial?

But we didn't waste time admiring these serving pieces for we hadn't eaten in fifteen hours. We began devouring our food.

There were many delicious types of fish along with other tasty dishes which I had

Dry Clothes and Food

never seen before and could not identify.

Once we had finished, we stretched out on some floor mats and were soon sound asleep.

I had no idea how long we slept, but I was awakened by the hissing of cool air blowing into the room. Ned and Conseil awoke soon after me, but Ned was still as angry as he had been the night before.

"Do you think they're going to keep us locked up in this iron box forever?" he shouted.

"I don't know any more than you do, Ned," I answered. "My guess is that we have stumbled upon a very important secret, namely this submarine! And if the captain wants to keep this secret, then our lives will not be important to him. If, however, this is not the case, then he will probably return us to dry land as soon as possible."

"But Professor," cried Ned, "we have to do something! We can't just sit and wait!"

Cool Air Wakes the Professor.

"Do what?" I asked, puzzled.

"Escape!"

"Escape from an underwater prison?" I cried. "That's impossible!"

"No, Professor," said Ned. "It's not impossible if we take over the ship!"

Arguing with Ned's wild plans wouldn't help our situation, so I simply tried to calm him by saying, "Let's wait and see what happens, Ned. Just try not to lose your temper or we'll never get the chance to do anything at all."

But as the hours went by with no sign of our cell door opening, Ned's anger increased. He paced back and forth like a wild animal in a cage. He kicked the iron walls and swore at the men outside. He shouted and yelled, but the steel walls were deaf!

I began to wonder just what kind of man this captain was. How could he lock us in here for so many hours and simply forget us?

Ned's Anger Increases.

Perhaps he wasn't the kind, courageous man I thought him to be. Perhaps he was nothing more than a cruel killer!

Just then, we heard footsteps on the metal floor outside. Bolts were pulled, the door opened, and the steward stepped into the room carrying a tray of food.

Before I could move, Ned rushed at the man. Dishes went flying as Ned knocked the steward to the floor and leaped on top of him. Ned's strong hands began choking him.

Conseil and I jumped on Ned and tried to loosen his grip on the half-conscious man. We struggled for several minutes until a voice above me froze me to the spot.

The voice spoke the following words in perfect English, "Calm down, Mr. Land!" Then, in perfect French, the voice added, "Thank you, Monsieur Conseil, and you, Professor Aronnax, for your help. And now, gentlemen, if you please, listen to me!"

Ned Attacks the Steward.

The Captain Speaks.

Chapter 4
Captain Nemo

It was the captain who had spoken!

Ned immediately jumped up and backed away from the gasping man on the floor.

"Gentlemen," said the captain, "I also speak French, English, German and Latin. So I could have answered you at our first meeting. But I wanted to take my time deciding what to do with you. After all, your cannons shot at me and Mr. Land tried to harpoon my ship. So I surely have the right to treat you as my enemies and kill you!"

"But that's not the act of a civilized man!" I

protested.

"Monsieur Aronnax," said the captain angrily, "I am *not* a civilized man. I have broken all ties with the civilized world on land. don't obey its rules. I make my own!"

I looked at the man with horror, but also with a little bit of curiosity.

"However," continued the captain more calmly, "I do have some feelings of pity, so I shall spare your lives. You will remain on board my ship forever as free men. You will have the freedom to walk about, to look, and even to examine everything that goes on here. You may do all this since you will never have the chance to tell what you have seen to another living soul!"

"But Monsieur," I cried, "you can't possibly expect us to give up our families, our friends, or our country forever!"

"Professor, giving up your life on land may not be as unpleasant as you think."

"I Am *Not* a Civilized Man."

"This is cruelty!" I cried.

"No, Monsieur, it is a kindness," replied the captain. "And I really do not have to be kind to you. You have discovered my secret—a secret the world was never to know. So I cannot permit you to go back and tell anyone that my ship or I exist!"

Then the captain seemed to relax and his voice became more gentle. "I know who you are, Monsieur Aronnax. I have been studying your great work on the ocean depths for many years, and I have great respect for you. Your knowledge is great, but you don't know everything. You haven't *seen* everything. I am offering you now the opportunity to see what no man on earth has ever seen—all the wonders of the ocean depths. You will accompany me on an underwater voyage around the world. During this voyage, you will discover the last secrets of our planet!"

The captain's words had a startling effect

An Invitation to an Underwater Voyage

on me! "Monsieur," I exclaimed, "my curios
ity as a scientist has just become stronge
than my desire for freedom! I shall b
honored to accompany you. But one last ques
tion, please. By what name shall I addres:
you, sir?"

"For you, Monsieur Aronnax, I shall be
simply Captain Nemo. You and your friends
are passengers on the *Nautilus*."

Captain *Nemo!* I thought. What a fitting
name for a man of mystery! *Nemo* in Latin
means *no man* or *nobody*. So I am talking
with Captain *Nobody!*

"And now, Monsieur Aronnax," said the
captain, smiling, "I'd be pleased if you would
lunch with me. Your friends will be shown to
their cabins where their meal awaits them."

I could hardly control my excitement as I
followed Captain Nemo along a narrow,
brightly-lit gangway. A door at the end
opened, and I found myself in a large,

Captain Nemo

richly-decorated dining room. Cabinets of fine wood held china, silver and glassware worth of any palace in Europe.

As we sat down, Captain Nemo explained. "All this food comes from the sea, for I no longer eat anything from the land. You will find it tasty and nourishing. Not only does the sea feed me, Professor, but it also clothes me and furnishes my ship. The cloth you are wearing was woven from the fine silky threads found in a certain type of oyster. Your bed is made out of soft eel grass. The pen on your desk is made out of whalebone and the ink comes from a squid."

The captain spoke with such enthusiasm that I, too, became carried away. "You love the sea, don't you, Captain!" I exclaimed.

"Yes, I love it! For only there, far below its surface, can a man be truly free!"

Free? Free from what? I wondered.

"All This Food Comes from the Sea."

Twelve Thousand Books

Chapter 5
The Remarkable *Nautilus*

After we finished lunch, we entered an adjoining room—a large library. I stared in wonder at the thousands of books lining the walls from floor to ceiling.

"Twelve thousand books, Monsieur Aronnax," said Captain Nemo. "Books on every subject and in every known language. And I have read them all! Please feel free to use any of them whenever you wish."

The man must be a genius, I thought as I began examining the shelves. In the center of the largest bookcase stood the one book which was probably the reason for the captain's friendliness to me. That book was *Mysteries of the Ocean Depths* by Pierre Aronnax

Just then, Captain Nemo opened a door at the far end of the room and called me to follow him. I entered a huge room filled with paintings, tapestries, and statues—all done by the greatest artists of the ancient and modern worlds. This room, the lounge, was truly a magnificent museum!

"These treasures are the last memories of my life on earth. That life is dead, but great art and great music live forever," he said pointing to a huge organ covered with sheets of music.

Besides the art and music, there were glass cases filled with collections of rare shells, colorful coral, priceless pearls, and other wonders of the ocean.

"My collection has great meaning for me," said Captain Nemo. "Everything you see has

Captain Nemo's Museum

been gathered from the sea by my own hands."

"No museum in the world has a collection like this! It must be worth millions!"

"You will be even more amazed, Professor, when I show you the wonders of the *Nautilus*. First, look at these instruments on the wall. These same instruments appear in every room on the ship. They tell me our exact position, our speed, the direction we are heading, and the weather on the surface."

"Remarkable!" I exclaimed. "But what puzzles me most, sir, is the power on the ship."

"Ah, Monsieur Aronnax, it is a mighty power, indeed. It gives me light and heat and runs all my machines. It is electricity!"

"But that's unheard of!" I cried in shock. "Our scientists on land have only been able to produce tiny sparks of electricity in their laboratories! We still use gas for our lights, and wood and coal for our heat. And we

Instruments on the *Nautilus*

certainly have no machines run by electric
motors! Where does this powerful electrical
energy come from, Captain?"

"Again from the sea, Professor. I remove
salt from the sea water and use it to charge
special batteries I've made. This gives me
power greater than any known in the world!"

"Amazing!" I cried. "And your air supply?"

"I renew the air on the ship simply by surfacing. However, I use electricity to operate
the pumps which store extra air in huge reservoirs. That way, the *Nautilus* can stay
submerged for several days."

My head was spinning as we left the cabin
and walked along a gangway. We came to a
companionway, a well-shaped opening. It had
a ladder going up. I asked where it led to.

"To the dinghy," replied Captain Nemo.

"What! You have a dinghy on board?"

"Yes, and it's a splendid little boat. We use
it when we want to go fishing."

The Ladder to the Dinghy

"Only when you're surfaced, of course?"

"Not at all! The hatch at the top of the ladder opens into a hatch in the dinghy. This little boat has a watertight cover. So once I am inside it, I simply undo the bolts holding it to the ship, and it shoots up to the surface. There, I lift the cover and the dinghy is ready to set sail."

We continued on to the engine room where Captain Nemo explained how he submerged the *Nautilus*, then brought her back to the surface. "Inside the ship are several water reservoirs. When they are filled with water, the ship gets heavier and submerges. Then, when I want to surface, I pump out this water and the ship rises."

"Amazing!" I cried. "But when you are underwater, how can you see to steer the ship?"

"There is a special glass compartment that sticks out on top of the ship. That is the

The Engine Room

helmsman's compartment. Behind that, i
another compartment, is a powerful electr:
light that illuminates the water for a mile."

"Aha!" I cried. "That explains the strang
glow that had everyone puzzled for month:
Sir, your *Nautilus* is truly amazing!"

"Yes, Professor. I love it as if it were m
own flesh and blood! For I am its designer
builder, and captain all in one."

"But how were you able to build thi
remarkable ship in secret?"

"Every part of it was made in a differen
country of the world, then sent to me at dif
ferent addresses, under different names. My
crew and I set up our workshop on a deser:
island and built the *Nautilus* there."

"All this must have cost a fortune!"

"Well over a million dollars, Professor! Bu:
that is a mere nothing to me. You see, Monsieur Aronnax, I am a billionaire!"

Could I really believe what this strange

The Strange Glow

man was telling me? I'd know soon enough.

We returned to the lounge, and Captain Nemo pointed to a large wall map. "We are now three hundred miles from Japan. It is exactly twelve noon on November 8, 1867. At this moment, we are beginning our under water voyage around the world!"

With that, Captain Nemo left the room. Just as I was about to leave too, all the lights in the lounge went out. I heard the noise of something sliding and saw two panels open. They revealed two windows—one on each side of the ship. The water outside was brightly lit for a mile around.

What a sight! I seemed to be looking through the windows of a huge aquarium! Never before had I been able to see all these creatures alive and free in their natural waters! I sat for hours, fascinated by the army of rare, colorful fish speeding by.

For the next eight days, I saw nothing of

A Huge Aquarium!

Captain Nemo. Ned, Conseil, and I were surprised at his mysterious absence. But we kept ourselves busy at the windows which were opened for us every day.

On the morning of the ninth day, a note was delivered to my cabin. It read:

16 November 1867

PROFESSOR ARONNAX:
I am pleased to invite you and your friends on a hunting expedition tomorrow in the forest of Crespo Island.

CAPTAIN NEMO

"A hunting expedition!" cried Ned. "That means we're going ashore. We can escape!"

If the captain hated dry land, why was he going hunting in a forest? I was puzzled by this, but I had the chance to ask Captain Nemo this question the following morning.

The captain smiled as he replied, "Professor, this forest is not on land. It is under water!"

An Invitation to Go Hunting

"Under water?" I asked in amazement.

"Yes, Professor, but you will stay perfectly dry while you are hunting."

I looked at the captain oddly. He's gone out of his mind, I thought.

My face must have revealed what I was thinking, for the captain chuckled. "No, Professor, I'm not mad! Surely you have seen diving suits before, you—a man of science."

"Yes, Captain, but the men in those suits were attached to their boats by long air hoses. Those hoses did not permit them to go far enough away to hunt."

"Aha! But Professor, I have developed a special air tank that is strapped onto a diver's back. With it, he can move about as freely as he wishes and even stay on the ocean floor for nine or ten hours!"

"Captain Nemo, that is truly remarkable!" I exclaimed. "I am ready to go on this hunting expedition. Wherever you go, I'll go too."

Captain Nemo's Special Air Tanks

Dressing for the Hunt

Chapter 6
Beneath the Pacific Ocean

"You mean we're not going on land to hunt?" cried Ned angrily. "Then I refuse to go!"

Conseil, however, followed me everywhere, so he fell in behind me as Captain Nemo led us to a small dressing room. Two crewmen helped us on with our heavy rubber waterproof diving suits and thick shoes weighted with lead. Next, they screwed large metal and glass helmets onto the threaded collars of our suits and strapped air tanks to our backs. We began to breathe easily. Last, they hooked electric lamps onto our belts and placed air guns in our hands. These guns shot tiny glass bullets containing powerful electrical charges.

We moved to a small compartment next to the dressing room, and a watertight door was sealed. Soon I felt cold water rising from my feet to my chest to my head. When the compartment was completely flooded, a door in the hull of the *Nautilus* opened. A moment later, Captain Nemo led us out onto the ocean floor.

We started walking along a sandy plain towards a group of rocks covered with many varieties and colors of zoophytes, which are tiny sea animals that look like plants and flowers. Overhead, schools of fish swam by. It was a marvelous feast for my eyes!

After we had been walking for an hour, the ground began to slope sharply downward. Ahead of us lay a narrow valley between two

The Compartment Floods.

high walls. This valley, five hundred feet beneath the surface, contained large treelike plants whose branches rose straight up. The valley floor was covered with sharp rocks and shadowy plants which did not flower in these dark depths of the ocean.

This, then, was the forest of Crespo Island. We went deeper into it for the next several hours until we came to a huge wall of rock—the edge of the island itself. This was as far as Captain Nemo would go, for this wall of rock was dry land, and he had sworn never to set foot on dry land again.

As we turned to head back to the *Nautilus*, Captain Nemo suddenly stopped and raised his gun. I heard a faint hissing sound and saw an animal fall dead a few feet away.

It was a magnificent sea otter whose brown and silver fur was worth hundreds of dollars on land. It was a strange-looking animal with its round head, short ears, catlike whiskers,

Captain Nemo Kills a Sea Otter.

clawed webbed feet, and furry tail. One of the crewmen lifted the five-foot-long creature on his shoulders and carried it with us back to the *Nautilus*.

Once we were inside the compartment, Captain Nemo pressed a button. The outside door closed and the pumps began lowering the water level. Soon the compartment was dry and we stepped into the dressing room.

During the days and weeks that followed, I hardly saw Captain Nemo. The panels in the lounge were kept open so Ned, Conseil, and I could watch the mysteries of underwater life. The first mate marked our position on the chart so I was able to follow our course. We had just passed the Hawaiian Islands and were heading southeast in the Pacific Ocean. We had already traveled 4,860 leagues, or 14,580 miles, from our starting point off the coast of Japan.

On the night of December 11, the *Nautilus*

Marking the Position of the *Nautilus*

lay motionless at a depth of 3,000 feet. I was in the lounge reading when Conseil called to me in a strange voice.

"Monsieur, please come to the window!"

I went over to where Conseil stood and saw an enormous black mass outside. Was it some kind of gigantic whale?. . .Then suddenly I realized. . ."A ship!" I cried.

"Yes, Professor," said Ned, who was also gazing out. "It's a sunken ship!"

It obviously had sunk only hours earlier for there hadn't even been time for any sea life to start clinging to it. It was a sad sight! But its deck was even sadder! Four men with their bodies twisted horribly were tied to the masts. A woman, half out of a hatch, was lifting a child over her head as its arms clutched her neck! The helmsman was frozen at the wheel of the ship, his hair stuck to his forehead by the water. He seemed to be steering his ghost ship through the ocean depths.

A Sunken Ship!

Our hearts were beating fast, but none of us could utter a word. Then I saw several huge sharks moving towards the wreck. The scent of human flesh blazed fire in their eyes.

The *Nautilus* sped away, but the three of us sat frozen for several hours afterwards.

On January 2, we entered Torres Strait—the body of water separating Australia from the island of New Guinea. Torres Strait is one of the most dangerous straits on earth to sail through, not only because of its reefs and rocks, but also because of the cannibals who live along its coast.

"What an awful stretch of water!" cried Ned as he, Conseil, and I stood on the platform on the deck of the *Nautilus*.

With Captain Nemo at the helm, however, the *Nautilus* cruised slowly past most of the terrible reefs. But just as we were nearing the end of the strait, a sudden blow knocked us off our feet. The *Nautilus* had struck a

The Dangerous Torres Strait

reef and had gone aground!

Captain Nemo came out onto the platform to reassure us that no damage had been done. However, we would be grounded on the reef until the tide rose. And that would be in five days when the full moon came out.

As soon as Captain Nemo went below, Ned exclaimed excitedly, "This is our chance to escape! We're only two miles from land."

"The land you see, Ned, is New Guinea," I replied. "And the natives are cannibals!"

"But couldn't we at least get over there and hunt some animals? I'm dying to sink my teeth into some meat after months of fish!"

I went below to ask Captain Nemo if we could go ashore to hunt and, to my great surprise, he agreed.

So the following morning, we loaded our guns and axes on the dinghy and set off. After two months at sea, we were overjoyed at being on dry land again!

Going Ashore to Hunt

We ran from tree to bush, picking and eating bananas, pineapples, coconuts, mangoes, cabbages, beans, and yams. We stuffed ourselves as much as we could, then loaded the rest of our supply on board the dinghy.

Then we returned to the forest to hunt for our main course—the meat.

By late afternoon, we came upon a wild boar which Ned killed with one shot. He then skinned it and cleaned it, cutting its meat into several fine chops.

We returned to the beach and soon had a fire going. Our roasting chops filled the air with a delicious smell. Even I had to admit how much I missed the taste of meat.

We sat down to start our feast. A chop was in my hand, halfway to my mouth, when a shower of stones and arrows came at us from the edge of the forest.

"It's the cannibals!" cried Conseil. "Head for the dinghy at once!"

The Cannibals Attack.

Fleeing New Guinea

Chapter 7
Strange Secrets on Board

Hundreds of savages were on our heels as we raced to the dinghy. Stones and arrows fell all around us as we jumped in and began rowing. Luckily, there were no canoes on shore in which the savages could follow us!

We reached the *Nautilus* safely, and I hurried below to find Captain Nemo. He was in the lounge, playing the magnificent organ.

"Ah, it's you, Professor," he said, looking up. "How was your hunting expedition?"

"We were attacked by savages!" I cried.

Captain Nemo didn't seem surprised.

"Anywhere you set foot on land, Professor, you will find savages—here, as well as in your part of the world."

"But what if they come out to attack us?"

Captain Nemo began playing again as he calmly answered, "Even if all the savages on New Guinea came out to attack us, the *Nautilus* would have nothing to fear."

Feeling a little more assured by the captain's words, I went to my cabin to rest.

At six the next morning, I went up to the platform and looked towards the shore. The sea was filled with dugout canoes and hundreds of savages paddling towards the ship.

I ran below to warn Captain Nemo. I knocked at his cabin door and rushed in.

"You are disturbing me," said Captain Nemo as he sat at his work table with piles of papers in front of him. "But I imagine you have some serious reason for doing so."

"Very serious sir," I said. "We're being

Attacking the *Nautilus*

attacked by hundreds of savages!"

"Oh?" said the captain calmly. "Then all we need do is close the hatches. See, I press this button and it's done. Surely, Professor, you can't think that these gentlemen could damage our hull with their arrows when the cannon balls from your warship could not even dent it."

Then he returned to his work and I to my cabin. All day and all night I could hear the savages walking about on the platform, letting out bloodcurdling yells.

At 2:30 the next afternoon, Captain Nemo came into the lounge and announced that the tide had risen and freed us from the reef. We would renew our air supply and set off.

"But what about the savages?" I asked. "Won't they come below when you open the hatch?"

"Monsieur Aronnax, no one can get down that hatch if I do not want them to. But of

Captain Nemo Isn't Worried.

course, you don't understand. Come with me!"

I followed the captain along the gangway to the ladder leading up to the hatch. We stood looking up as the hatch sprang open. Immediately, twenty horrible faces glared down at us. One of the savages grabbed onto the ladder to start down, but he was thrown back by some strange force. He ran off cursing and jumping about wildly.

Ten more savages tried grabbing the ladder and ran off screaming the same way.

I realized then that this was not just a plain iron ladder. It was an electrically charged one! And anybody touching it against the captain's wishes would get a powerful shock. No wonder they ran off screaming!

And so the *Nautilus*, free of savages and freed from the reef, began moving once again.

Two weeks later, we were in the Indian Ocean, six hundred miles west of Australia.

A Powerful Electric Shock!

One morning when we surfaced for air, I went up on the platform. The first mate was there scanning the horizon as he did every morning. Suddenly, he called down the hatch in an excited voice. Almost instantly, Captain Nemo appeared on deck. He began looking at something on the horizon through his telescope.

I put my own telescope to my eye, but before I had the chance to focus the lens, it was abruptly snatched out of my hands.

I turned around and saw Captain Nemo standing before me. His eyes were flashing angrily, his body was rigid, and his fists were clenched. But he wasn't looking at me. He was gazing at something on the horizon.

After several minutes, his usual calm returned and he spoke. "Monsieur Aronnax, I must lock you and your companions in the cell for a while."

"Can you tell me why?" I asked, puzzled.

Captain Nemo Grabs the Telescope.

"No, Monsieur, I cannot!"

Five minutes later, Ned, Conseil, and I found ourselves locked in the cell where we had spent our first night on board. Our lunch was brought in, and since we had nothing else to do, we ate. Ned and Conseil ate well, but I only picked at my food. I was much too confused to think of eating!

No sooner had Ned and Conseil finished their meal than they put their heads down on the table and fell into a deep sleep. I felt my brain become drowsy, but I tried hard to keep my eyes open. A painful thought suddenly crossed my mind—some sort of sleeping powder had been mixed with our food! Locking us in this cell wasn't enough to keep us from knowing Captain Nemo's secrets. We had to be put to sleep too!

My eyelids closed like lead weights. I fell into a deathlike sleep filled with wild terrifying dreams!

Drugged!

Captain Nemo Looks Tired and Sad.

Chapter 8
The Coral Cemetery

The next morning I awoke to find myself back in my cabin. My door was unlocked, and I assumed I was no longer a prisoner. So I gathered up my scientific notes and went into the lounge to work on them.

I saw nothing of Captain Nemo until he entered the lounge later in the afternoon. His red eyes showed that he had not slept at all the night before, and his whole face had a look of sadness on it—a look I had never seen there before.

After pacing back and forth for several

minutes, he came over to me and asked, "Are you a doctor, Monsieur Aronnax?"

"Why yes!" I answered in surprise. "I practiced for several years before starting my work at the Paris Museum."

"Well then, would you mind treating one of my men?"

"Certainly!" I answered and followed him to a cabin in the crew's quarters.

There, stretched out on a bed was a man of about forty, with a strong rugged face. His head was wrapped in bloodstained bandages. I removed the bandages and examined the wound. It was horrible! The skull had been smashed by some hard instrument and part of the brain was exposed. The blood had already clotted and turned to a dark red. The man's breathing was very slow, his pulse was weak, and his arms and legs were cold. I realized that death was near.

There was nothing I could do for him.

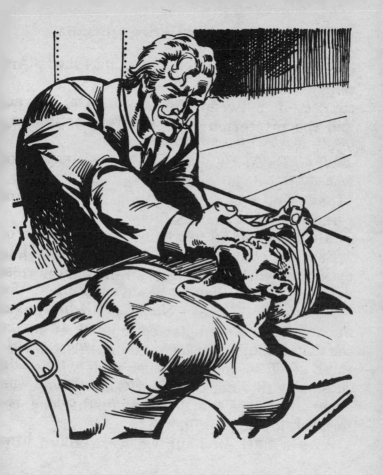

Treating a Wounded Crewman

except to put a fresh bandage on his head. But I couldn't help but wonder if there was some connection between this wounded crewman and the mysterious events of the night before!

When I asked Captain Nemo how the man was wounded, he answered me very sharply. "That is no business of yours! I'm only concerned with his chances."

"He'll be dead in two hours," I said.

Captain Nemo clenched his fists and his eyes filled with tears. How strange to see this man cry! I never believed he could.

I didn't see Captain Nemo again until the next morning. I had started to ask him about the dying man when he broke in, inviting the three of us to go on another underwater excursion with him. Ned and Conseil were so eager to say yes that I had no further chance to speak to the captain.

Within half an hour we were all in our

"He'll Be Dead in Two Hours."

diving suits, stepping out on the ocean floor.
Captain Nemo led the way and a dozen crew
members followed behind us.

A gentle slope led us ninety feet below the
surface, where I got my first glimpse of the
coral kingdom.

Coral is the skeleton of a tiny, jellylike sea
animal called a polyp. These polyps live in
colonies, and their skeletons slowly build one
upon the other, sometimes forming reefs and
islands.

Here, the coral formed a stone forest beneath the sea. Thick shrubs and trees made
of this rocklike coral were covered with
thousands of colorful flowerlike polyps. I
reached out to pick one of these living flowers, but as my hand drew near, an alarm
seemed to spread through the entire colony.
The white blossoms darted inside their red
cases and vanished from sight. The flowering
shrub turned into a bumpy, stony tree.

The Coral Kingdom

We continued heading downhill until w
reached a depth of a thousand feet. Here, th
coral formed stone trees connected to eac
other by beautifully colored vines. Beneat
our feet, smaller varieties of coral formed
carpet of flowers that shone like dazzlin
jewels!

In the middle of this magnificent garde
was a circular clearing. Mounds of sand wer
piled up in several places around a larg
coral cross. These mounds had definitely bee
formed by the hands of man, not by the sea.

Captain Nemo stopped at this clearing, an
his crew formed a half circle around him. A
a sign from their captain, two crewme
stepped forward and began digging a long hol
When they were finished, four other men ap
proached the hole carrying a long white bun
dle on their shoulders.

Suddenly I understood! Captain Nemo an
his men had come to bury their shipmate i

Digging a Grave in the Coral Kingdom

their own private cemetery on the ocean floor.

As soon as the body was placed in its grave and covered over, Captain Nemo and his men knelt down to pray. Ned, Conseil, and I knelt too.

After several minutes with our heads bowed, the funeral procession started back to the *Nautilus*.

Once we were on board, Captain Nemo explained that the wounded man had died during the night. "We have buried him in our peaceful cemetery," he said. "The coral will now seal his grave forever!"

"At least there, Captain, your dead can sleep quietly, beyond the reach of sharks."

"Yes," Captain Nemo replied bitterly, "beyond the reach of sharks and men!"

A Funeral on the Ocean Floor

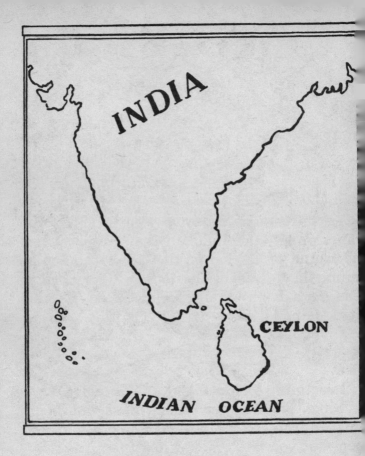

The Island of Ceylon

Chapter 9
Pearls and Sharks!

February began and we were almost half-way through the Indian Ocean, approaching the island of Ceylon at the tip of the Indian peninsula. I was in the lounge one morning reading a book about Ceylon when Captain Nemo joined me.

"Ceylon is famous for its pearl fisheries," he said. "Would you like to visit one of them?"

"I certainly would, Captain," I replied.

"Fine! The fishing season does not begin until March, so we will not see any fishermen, but you will enjoy it just the same."

"How do these fishermen bring up th
pearl oysters?" I asked.

"Their methods are quite primitive, I'
afraid. The divers go down about forty fee
while attached to their boats by a rope.
heavy stone gripped between their feet hol
them down as they gather the oysters."

"But how long can these divers stay dow
without any kind of diving suit or air?"

"Not too long," answered the captain
"Some manage to stay down about a minut
but when these poor creatures return to th
surface, blood is usually pouring out of thei
ears and noses from the pressure of the wa
ter. That is, *if* they come up. For there is al
ways the danger of sharks in these waters!"

"Sharks!" I exclaimed. "Will we be facin
sharks?"

"It's quite possible, Professor! But you'
find shark hunting very interesting too."

Once Captain Nemo left the room, I brok

An Indian Pearl Diver

out into a cold sweat. Sharks! I wiped m
forehead and picked up my book on Ceylc
again. I tried to concentrate on the word
but between every line, I kept seeing the te
rifying wide-open jaws of sharks!

Just then, Ned and Conseil burst in.

"We have received a pleasant invitatic
from that captain of yours!" exclaimed Ned.

"Oh?" I said. "So you know. . ."

"Yes," answered Conseil, "the captain h
invited us to visit the magnificent pea
fisheries of Ceylon."

"Did he tell you anything else?" I asked.

"Only that it will be very interesting," sa
Conseil.

I realized that Captain Nemo had not to
them about the sharks. Should I?. . .But ;
that moment, Conseil asked me how oyste
made pearls, and I was grateful for th
chance to take my mind off sharks for
while. So I began my lesson on pearls.

Thinking About Sharks

"The oyster is a small sea animal with two shells covering its soft flesh. Sometimes a tiny sea creature or a grain of sand finds its way inside these two shells and rubs against the oyster's flesh. To protect itself, the oyster forms a hard covering over this object. Layer upon layer of this covering is built up over a period of years, and a shark is formed."

"A shark?" cried Ned.

"Did I say shark? I meant pearl, of course!"

"Does an oyster ever contain more than one pearl?" asked Conseil.

"Yes, my boy. Some oysters have contained several sharks."

"You mean pearls!" exclaimed Conseil.

"Yes, of course, pearls! By the way, are you gentlemen afraid of sharks?"

"Me?" answered Ned. "A longtime harpooner? It's part of my job to laugh at them!"

"I'm not talking about harpooning them from the deck of a ship," I explained.

Pearls Grow inside Oysters.

"You mean we're going to..." But Ned couldn't finish his question.

"That's right," I said, "underwater! And what about you, Conseil?"

"If Monsieur is willing to face sharks, then his faithful servant will face them too."

The next morning we sat in silence as the crew rowed the dinghy towards the oyster beds. We were about three miles from shore when Captain Nemo gave the order to drop anchor. As we were putting on our diving suits, Captain Nemo handed me a steel knife.

"This will be more useful to you down there than a gun!" he said.

Ned and Conseil had knives too. In addition, Ned carried an enormous harpoon!

The crew helped us over the side of the dinghy, and we followed Captain Nemo along the ocean floor. Pearl oysters by the millions clung to rocks all around us. We were all anxious to begin filling our sacks with these

A Useful Weapon

treasures that just might contain pearls.

Just then, Captain Nemo motioned for us to squat down behind a rock. He pointed to a spot about fifteen feet away where a shadowy figure with a stone between his feet was descending to the ocean floor.

It was a diver, probably an Indian, come in search of pearls before the regular harvest time. We watched him dive several times, drop to his knees, fill his sack with oysters, then swim up to his boat.

Suddenly, while he was in the midst of tearing an oyster from the rock to which it was attached, a look of terror came over his face. When I saw a gigantic shadow appear above him, I understood his terror. A huge shark was heading towards him with its jaws wide open!

I was frozen to the spot where I crouched. As the shark headed in for the kill, the Indian jumped to one side and avoided its jaws.

The Pearl Diver Is Terrified.

But the shark's powerful tail struck him on the chest and knocked him flat on the ocean floor.

Then, just as the shark was getting ready to cut the Indian in two, Captain Nemo jumped up. With his knife raised, he headed straight for the monster, ready to fight it hand to hand.

The shark, seeing another possible victim, turned to attack the captain. When it was just inches away, Captain Nemo stepped to the side and buried his knife in the animal's belly. Blood poured from the wound and the sea turned red.

But the shark still had some fight left in it. The brave captain clutched one of its fins and plunged his knife into the creature's belly again and again. But he couldn't seem to strike its heart and kill it.

Then suddenly, the creature pushed its enormous weight against the captain and

Captain Nemo Fights the Shark.

knocked him to the ground. The shark's jaws opened, ready to cut the captain in two. But at that instant, Ned leaped forward and hurled his harpoon. The shark thrashed about with terrifying fury, then it was still. Ned had struck its heart!

Captain Nemo got up immediately and went over to the Indian. He took him in his arms and swam up to the surface with him.

The three of us followed them up to the fisherman's boat. Captain Nemo gave the man artificial respiration, and he soon opened his eyes. How surprised he must have been to see four helmets bending over him! But he must have been even more surprised when Captain Nemo put a bag of pearls into his trembling hands. Where had his luck come from?

We then left the puzzled Indian and made our way back to the dinghy.

The moment Captain Nemo's helmet was

Ned Attacks!

removed, he turned to Ned and said, "Thank you for saving my life, Mr. Land."

As the dinghy sped back to the *Nautilus,* we saw the dead body of the shark floating on the surface. It was well over twenty-five feet long, and its huge mouth, with six rows of teeth, took up one-third of its body!

Within minutes, a dozen other sharks appeared and began fighting over the flesh of the dead shark.

Back on board the *Nautilus,* I felt the need to tell Captain Nemo how much I admired his courage and his deep concern for another human being.

When he answered, it was in a trembling voice. "This Indian lives in a land where his people are abused by others. His kind of people are the ones I shall help till the day I die!"

A Meal for Other Sharks

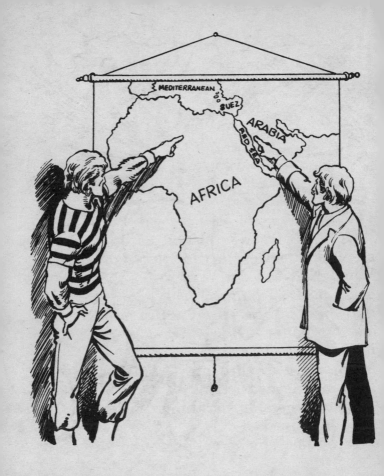

"The Red Sea Is a Dead End!"

Chapter 10
An Undersea Tunnel

Once Ceylon was behind us, the *Nautilus* steered due west across the Arabian Sea. When Ned saw our course on the map, he exclaimed, "Professor, we're heading right into the Red Sea. And the Red Sea is a dead end! Perhaps, one day when the Suez Canal is finished, we'll be able to reach the Mediterranean through it, but the canal is still under construction!"

"Then where do you think Captain Nemo is heading?" I asked.

"Who knows where?" answered Ned with a

shrug. "All I know is we've been prisoners here for three months. It's got to end!"

"Ned," I said calmly, "this is not yet the time to think of escape. Perhaps when we get closer to European waters..."

But Ned didn't let me finish. He left the room, muttering, "A man can't go on like this, living without his freedom."

I looked at the map again. Why *was* Captain Nemo taking us into the Red Sea when there was no way out but the way we had come in? I had no answers, so I simply made good use of my time observing the sea through the crystal-clear waters.

I saw marvelous shrubs of dazzling coral and huge rocks covered with a green fur of seaweed. How many new types of colorful fish, flowers and plants appeared before me!

At noon on February 9, we were cruising on the surface when Captain Nemo came up to the platform. "Well, Professor," he said,

Wonders Beneath the Red Sea

"how are you enjoying the wonders of the Red Sea?"

"The *Nautilus* is a remarkable boat for such a study," I replied. "It certainly is centuries ahead of its time. What a pity that such a secret will one day die with its inventor!"

Captain Nemo gave me an icy stare but said nothing. I thought it best to change the subject, so I asked him if he had ever been in the Red Sea before.

"Yes, Monsieur," he replied, "all the way up to the northern end where the Suez Canal is being built."

"And will the *Nautilus* be able to use the canal once it's finished?" I asked.

"I'm afraid I cannot risk having the *Nautilus* seen. However, the canal will be very useful to the rest of the world by connecting the Mediterranean to the Red Sea and then to the Indian Ocean. Your country-

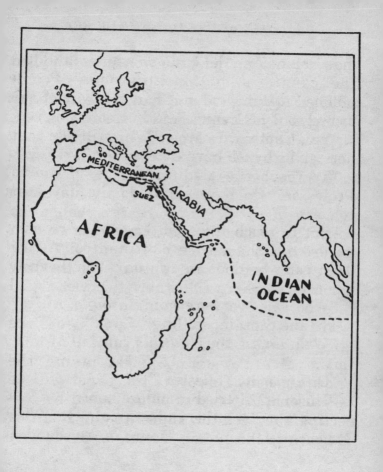

A Useful Canal Through Suez

man, Monsieur deLesseps, who is building the canal, is an amazing man! People laughed at him and stood in the way of this project, but his genius finally won!"

"Yes, Captain, I agree. But I still don't understand why *we* have entered the Red Sea."

"To reach the Mediterranean, of course, Professor, which we shall do the day after tomorrow."

"But to reach the Mediterranean, we must go *around* the entire continent of Africa! That can't be done in two days, not even by the *Nautilus*."

"Who said we were going *around* Africa?" asked the captain, smiling.

"Well, unless the *Nautilus* can sail over dry land. . . ."

"Or under it, Professor?"

"Under it?" I cried in amazement.

"Yes," replied the captain calmly. "What Monsieur deLesseps is doing on the land at

"We Must Go *Around* Africa."

Suez—digging a passage—nature has already done below the ocean floor!"

"You mean there's an underground passage at Suez?" I gasped.

"Yes," said the captain. "I call it the Arabian Tunnel. You see, Monsieur Aronnax, the land at Suez is covered with sand. But this sand is only one hundred fifty feet deep. Below it is a layer of solid rock. In this rock nature has made the tunnel."

"I can hardly believe my ears, Captain. How did you ever discover this tunnel?"

"On my early trips in this area, I noticed that the Red Sea and the Mediterranean contained identical types of fish. This made me wonder if perhaps there was some passage between the two seas for the fish to get through. If such a passage did exist, the water would have to flow from the Red Sea into the Mediterranean because the water level is higher in the Red Sea. So I searched

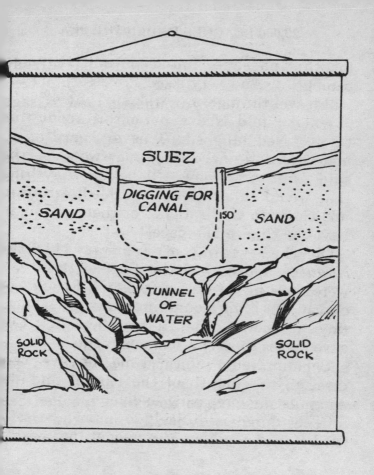

The Arabian Tunnel

for this passage, found it, and traveled through it. And very soon, Professor, you too will travel through my Arabian Tunnel!"

When I told Ned and Conseil about this tunnel, Ned laughed. "I never heard of an underwater tunnel connecting two seas," he said, "but right now, I'll believe anything that would take us into the Mediterranean and closer to civilization. For then, we might have the chance to escape!"

On the evening of February 11, the *Nautilus* approached the Gulf of Suez. We were cruising on the surface, and I could see clearly the high mountain known in biblical times as Mount Sinai. It was there that God gave Moses the Ten Commandments!

Captain Nemo informed me that we were close to the mouth of the tunnel and the *Nautilus* was preparing to dive.

"The tunnel is difficult to enter," he said, "so I stay at the helm throughout that part o

The Biblical Mount Sinai

the voyage. Perhaps, Monsieur Aronnax, you would like to watch from the helmsman's compartment as I steer through the tunnel."

"I would be very honored," I answered.

We entered a compartment about six feet square. Through the thick glass I saw high walls only a few feet from either side of us. Captain Nemo didn't take his eyes off these walls for an instant.

Soon I heard a strange rumbling sound. It was the sound of water rushing down the sloping tunnel from one sea into the other. This current sent the *Nautilus* shooting forward at an unbelievable rate of speed. For twenty minutes, my heart beat excitedly as the narrow walls of the tunnel sped by.

Then we gradually slowed down. Captain Nemo finally turned to me and said, "Professor, the Mediterranean!"

The *Nautilus* Shoots Through the Tunnel.

Ned Wants to Have a Chat.

Chapter 11
Through the Mediterranean

When the *Nautilus* surfaced the next morning, I rushed up to the platform for my first look at the Mediterranean. Ned and Conseil listened as I described our trip through the tunnel.

"Okay, I'm impressed, Professor," said Ned. "But now that we're in the Mediterranean, it's time for us to have a little chat."

I knew what Ned wanted to chat about— escaping! I realized how badly he wanted his freedom, but the scientist in me wanted to stay on board the *Nautilus*. I had almost finished rewriting my book on underwater life, and I was doing it in the middle of the very places I was describing! Where would I ever find another chance to see these wonders of the ocean again?

"I'm sure we'll get an opportunity to escape," I said. "Why not wait till we're nearer to France or England or America?"

"But we're near civilized countries right now," said Ned. "We may not get the chance later!"

"I guess you're right," I admitted with a sigh. "But the opportunity must be a good one. If our first attempt doesn't succeed, we won't get a second one. Captain Nemo will see to that!"

"The best time will be some dark night when the *Nautilus* gets near the coast of Europe," said Ned.

"I don't think you can count on Captain Nemo getting close to any coast," I said. "You

Professor Aronnax Wants to Wait.

know how he feels about dry land."

Events of the next few days proved how true my words were. We cruised underwater far from any shore most of the time. Was it because Captain Nemo suspected what we might do? Or did he simply want to stay out of sight of the many ships that sailed the Mediterranean?

Our first afternoon in the Mediterranean, we were in the general area of the island of Crete. Just before leaving America, I had read about an uprising by the Cretans against their cruel Turkish rulers. But being at sea all these months, I had no way of knowing how this uprising turned out.

Captain Nemo spent most of the day pacing back and forth in the lounge where I was writing. Towards evening, the panels, which had been closed all day, were suddenly opened. I busied myself studying the fish, but Captain Nemo seemed to be looking beyond

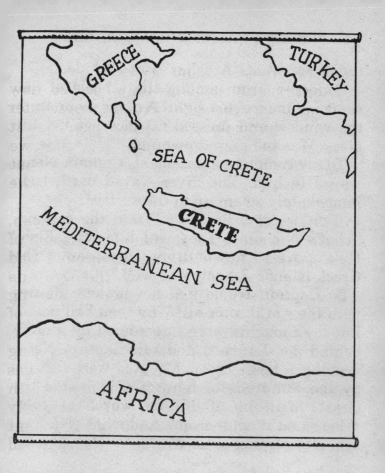

The Island of Crete

them. For what? At what? I had no idea!

Suddenly, from among the schools of fish came an unexpected sight! A diver swam up to the window and pressed his face against the glass. Was the man drowning?

To my complete amazement, Captain Nemo waved to him. The diver waved back, then immediately swam up to the surface.

"Don't worry, Professor," said the captain. "That's Nicholas. They call him 'The Fish.' He's a well-known diver throughout the Greek Islands. I know him well."

So Captain Nemo had not broken all ties with the world after all! Why then had he. . .? But my thoughts were interrupted by a noise behind me. I turned and saw Captain Nemo opening a large chest. My eyes were dazzled by the hundreds of bars of gold inside the chest. Millions of dollars worth of gold! Where had it come from? And what was Captain Nemo going to do with it?

"Millions of Dollars Worth of Gold!"

I stood dumbfounded as four crewmen entered and began pushing the heavy chest out of the lounge. Soon, I heard some pulleys in the companionway lifting the chest up to the hatch. Then the *Nautilus* surfaced.

Captain Nemo turned to me, said good night, and left the room.

The next day, we sped underwater through the Mediterranean at an unbelievable rate of speed—300 miles per hour! Trying to surface the dinghy and escape at that speed would have been suicide. So Ned's plans had to wait.

What little I saw of the Mediterranean's depths shocked me. Instead of the beauties of nature, I gazed at horrifying scenes of shipwrecks. Raging storms and dangerous reefs had been sending ships to their watery graves in this sea ever since ancient times.

That night, we left the grim Mediterranean behind us and entered the Atlantic Ocean.

Grim Wrecks Beneath the Mediterranean

Escape in Such a Rough Sea?

Chapter 12
Captain Nemo's Treasure

When we surfaced for air the following morning, we were in the Atlantic about twelve miles off the coast of Spain.

Ned cornered me alone on the platform and whispered, "Our opportunity has come! Tonight at nine, we'll escape! You are to wait in the library until you get my signal."

"But the sea is quite rough," I said, hoping desperately to change his mind.

"I know," said Ned, "but that's the risk we'll have to take. For all we know, by tomorrow, the *Nautilus* might be hundreds of miles out to sea. Till tonight, Professor!"

With that, Ned left. What could I have said? He was right! There was no doubt about that. Captain Nemo would never let us go willingly. And this was a good opportunity, so close to shore.

I spent the rest of the day pacing in my cabin. I ate very little when the steward brought in my meals. My heart beat rapidly as the clock ticked away the hours. Suddenly, when it struck eight, I realized I had to get ready.

I dressed myself warmly in my sealskin coat, otter-skin cap, and sea boots. My notes were safely tucked inside my coat and I was ready.

At a few minutes before nine, I tiptoed through the lounge and into the library. I waited near the door leading to the gangway. Where was Ned's signal?

Suddenly, I heard the propeller stop and

Professor Aronnax Prepares to Leave.

felt a slight bump. The *Nautilus* had come to rest on the ocean floor. I became uneasy. What had gone wrong? There was no signal from Ned, and I wondered if he. . . .

Just then, the door opened and Captain Nemo entered. He asked me to follow him into the lounge. My legs were weak and my hands trembled as I obeyed him. Had he discovered our plan? Where were Ned and Conseil? What was he about to do with me?

The darkness in the lounge hid my fear from the captain. I was grateful for that. He led me to the panels and quickly opened them. The sea was lit up all around us, revealing a graveyard of old wrecked ships.

Several members of the crew in their diving suits were walking among the wrecks, lifting open chests, and scooping up objects from the ocean floor. I looked closer and discovered that these objects were coins, jewels, and bars of gold and silver!

Treasure on the Ocean Floor

One after another, the crewmen brought their treasures back to the *Nautilus*, then returned to the ocean floor for more.

"Professor," said Captain Nemo, "you seem stunned! Perhaps I can explain. We are now at Vigo Bay on the western coast of Spain. Back in 1702, a fierce battle was fought here between the English and the Spanish. Ships belonging to the Spanish king were returning from South America filled with treasures for him. But when the battle turned in favor of the English, the admiral of the Spanish fleet refused to let all the treasures fall into enemy hands. So he set fire to all twenty-three of his ships and let them sink to the ocean floor, taking all their treasures with them."

"And since you have found them, Captain, these treasures now belong to you?"

"Yes, Monsieur. I have picked up what other men have lost, not only here in Vigo

The Battle of Vigo Bay

Bay, but at thousands of other shipwrecks around the world. Now do you understand, Professor, how I came to be a billionaire?"

"But this wealth belongs to other men, to other countries!" I protested.

"Do you think I use this wealth for myself, Professor?" he snapped angrily. "What makes you think I don't make good use of it? Don't you think I know that people are suffering on earth, poor people to be helped, victims to be avenged? Don't you think I. . . ."

Captain Nemo stopped. Perhaps he regretted talking so freely. But his outburst was enough to convince me that he was truly a man with feelings for others—a man who helped suffering and enslaved people all over the world!

And then I understood where those gold bars were headed when they were unloaded near the island of Crete! It was to help the Cretans fight for their freedom!

"I Don't Use This Wealth for Myself!"

"We're Hundreds of Miles from Any Land."

Chapter 13
A Lost Continent

"That darned captain would have to stop the ship just as we were about to leave!" Ned muttered angrily the next day.

"Yes, Ned," I replied, "he had to see his banker."

"His banker?" Ned looked puzzled.

"Or rather his bank!" I then told him the story of the treasure at Vigo Bay.

"Well, everything's not over yet!" he said.

"For now it is!" I cried. "Look at the map! We're hundreds of miles from any land."

I must admit I was rather pleased still to

be on board the *Nautilus*, and I returned to my work eagerly. But I was even more pleased that night when I received an unexpected visit in my cabin from Captain Nemo.

"Professor," he said, "you have seen the ocean depths so far only in daylight. How would you like to see them now at night?"

"Very much, Captain," I replied, rather curious about this new excursion on which only I was invited.

Within minutes we were in our diving suits, walking on the ocean floor a thousand feet beneath the dark Atlantic.

It was almost midnight. The water was completely black, but Captain Nemo pointed to a reddish glow about two miles away from us. As we walked towards the glow, the flat ground started to rise and become quite rocky. The strange thing about these rocks was that they were laid out in a regular pattern—almost like a man-made road! I had

A Strange Underwater Glow

no way of questioning Captain Nemo about it for I didn't know the sign language he used with his crew underwater.

We were actually climbing a mountain, and the reddish glow was lighting up the whole area as we got closer to it. Captain Nemo pushed through the rocks and the forest of dead trees turned to stone like a man who had traveled this path many times.

When we reached the top, I looked out into the distance. There, unbelievable as it may seem, stood an underwater volcano! Its large crater was spitting out torrents of lava, giving the water its reddish glow.

As my eyes traveled to the base of the volcano, I was stunned to see a ruined, crumbled town. Its roofs were caved in, its temples were fallen, and its columns were lying on the ground. Off to one side lay the remains of a dock and parts of a ship. Further on were long lines of crumbled walls and deserted

A Volcano and an Ancient City

streets. Here was an entire city buried beneath the sea!

What part of the world had been swallowed up like this? I had to know! I tugged at Captain Nemo's sleeve and pointed. He picked up a stone, went over to a black rock, and wrote a single word—ATLANTIS.

Suddenly, everything became clear. This was the ancient continent which once stretched from Africa to America. It was supposedly struck by a giant earthquake and, in a single day, it sank into the sea.

Many historians believed Atlantis was only a legend, but here I was, standing on a mountain of this lost continent, touching ruins thousands of centuries old! Would this volcano one day bring these sunken ruins back to the surface again? And would this miracle of the past be revealed to man? My head was spinning with these thoughts as we returned to the *Nautilus*.

Atlantis, the Lost Continent!

Ned Wants to Hunt Whales.

Chapter 14
The South Pole

I spent weeks at my notes detailing all the wonders of Atlantis. But one day, Ned burst in and announced that we had just passed the tip of South America without turning west into the Pacific! We were still heading south, but south meant the icy wastelands of Antarctica and the South Pole!

We ran up on deck to ask Captain Nemo. Just as we climbed out of the hatch, Ned spied a herd of whales a mile from the ship.

"Can I go out and hunt them, Captain?" he asked. "Just to keep my harpoon in practice."

"Mr. Land," replied the captain coldly, "those are kind, playful black whales. They have enough trouble surviving attacks from their natural enemies, the sperm whales. They don't need you getting into the act!"

Ned's face turned purple with rage, but the captain ignored him as he went on. "The black whales are going to be in trouble soon enough. Look at those dots behind them."

We turned and looked out to sea.

"Those, gentlemen," said Captain Nemo, "are the cruel, destructive sperm whales! People have a right to kill them. And that is precisely what the *Nautilus* will do with the steel spur on her prow."

We went below and the *Nautilus* dove. Ned, Conseil, and I took our places at the window while Captain Nemo went to the helmsman's compartment to lead the attack.

The *Nautilus* became a fierce weapon in the hands of Captain Nemo as he plunged its

Black Whales Are Not for Hunting.

steel spur into whale after whale, cutting each one into two twisting halves. The battle raged for hours, then the sea was calm.

The *Nautilus* surfaced, and we rushed up on deck. The sea was covered with cut apart bodies floating in an ocean of blood!

As February turned into March, and we continued heading south, we began to see icebergs. But we steered between them until they became joined together by ice fields— long, unbroken plains of solid ice. For a while, the *Nautilus* was able to split the ice fields open with her strong prow. But finally, on March 18, we could go no further. We were up against a chain of ice mountains whose sharp peaks rose like thin needles three hundred feet into the air!

"It's the Great Ice Barrier!" cried Ned.

And truly it was. It was the one obstacle that no ship had ever been able to get through. We would have to turn back!

The Great Ice Barrier!

But as I looked back, I saw that that was impossible too! All the passages behind us had frozen together, closing us in.

"We're trapped, Captain!" I cried.

"Oh, Professor," said the captain calmly "you always worry. Not only will the *Nautilus* free herself, but she will continue on and take us to the South Pole. We shall discover the Pole together. Where others have failed, I, Captain Nemo, shall succeed!"

"I'd like to believe you, Captain," I replied "but do you plan to put wings on the *Nautilus* and fly over the Great Ice Barrier?"

"No, Professor! Not over it under it!"

Suddenly I realized that this just might be possible! For every foot of iceberg *above* water, there are three feet *below*. So, these three-hundred-foot-high ice mountains only went down nine hundred feet below the surface. And nine hundred feet was a mere nothing for the *Nautilus* to dive!

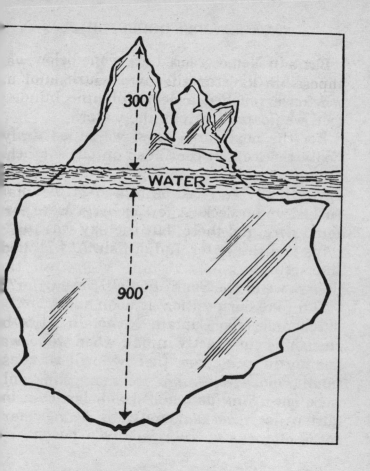

An Iceberg, Above and Below

Captain Nemo ordered everyone below, an the *Nautilus* started down. Sure enough when we reached a depth of nine hundre feet, we floated freely in the water.

For the next three days, we sailed under neath the ice, but continued on our southerl course.

We finally surfaced on March 21. All of u rushed up on deck. A few icebergs were sca tered here and there, but the sky was full birds and the water, full of fish. At 37° it fe like spring!

"Are we at the South Pole?" I asked.

"I'll take our position at noon and know fc sure," answered Captain Nemo. "If, at noo the sun is cut exactly in half when we look the northern horizon, then we will be at th South Pole."

So the *Nautilus* cruised slowly along th surface for several hours until we reached mass of rocks surrounded by a beach. Th

Surfacing near the South Pole

dinghy was put to sea and Captain Nemo, Conseil, and I got in. We rowed towards the sandy shore swarming with penguins, seals, and walruses.

"Monsieur," I said to Captain Nemo, "if this is the South Pole, you should have the honor of being the first to set foot on it!"

"Yes, Professor," he said, "and the only reason I'm setting foot on dry land is because no other human being has been here before."

Captain Nemo then jumped out of the dinghy and climbed up on a rock. Conseil and I waited several minutes, then followed.

I checked my watch. It was noon.

Captain Nemo lifted his telescope and pointed it to the north. Then he announced solemnly: "Today, March 21, 1868, I, Captain Nemo, reached the South Pole. I now take possession of this part of the world!"

Then he unrolled a black flag with a gold N on it and planted it in the rock!

Taking Possession of the South Pole

The *Nautilus* Heads North Again.

Chapter 15
Trapped Beneath the Ice

We now had to make plans for leaving, since March 21 was the beginning of the long polar night. It would be another six months before the sun shone here again.

The *Nautilus'* air tanks were filled and it slowly sank beneath the surface. We began heading north again.

At three o'clock the next morning, a violent blow threw me out of bed. The ship was leaning on its side, but I managed to crawl into the lounge. Ned and Conseil were there.

We sat stunned for several minutes until

Captain Nemo came rushing in.

"Have we had an accident?" I asked.

"Yes, Monsieur, an accident of nature. It seems that an enormous iceberg has turned over. As its base rose up, it trapped us between that base and the underside of the ice on the surface. We are in a kind of ice tunnel, Professor, but the *Nautilus* can still get out by moving forward or backward."

Just then, the propeller started up and we were underway, traveling forward at high speed. But two hours later, the *Nautilus* collided with something ahead. It was a wall of ice! There was not enough room in the tunnel to turn around, so the engines were reversed, and we began moving backward.

For three hours, the *Nautilus* sped south through the ice tunnel, but at 8:00 A.M., a second collision took place.

Captain Nemo entered the lounge in his diving suit and explained, "Our route to the

Inside a Tunnel of Ice

south is now blocked too. The iceberg has closed off every opening. But we shall not die without trying everything possible first. We still have a three-day supply of air, and we shall breathe it as we try cutting ourselves out through the walls of ice."

Ned then spoke up. "Captain Nemo, I'm as good with a pickax as I am with a harpoon!"

"Thank you, Mr. Land," said the captain. "We shall need everyone's help! My men and I have just been checking the thickness of the ice outside. Above us, it is 1,300 feet thick, on the sides, 50 feet thick, and below us, 30 feet thick. Therefore, we shall start digging a trench on the floor of the ice off to the side of the ship."

Ned left with the captain to join the first group at work. After two hours, Conseil and I joined the second group.

We alternated shifts for the next twelve hours, but we were able to remove only three

Every Opening Is Closed Off.

feet of ice. If work continued at this rate, we would need five nights and four days to cut through the ice. But we only had two days of air left in the reservoirs!

And then, even if we managed to dig ourselves free, who knew how long it would be until we could surface and get fresh air?

By the next day, the ice overhead and on the sides of the tunnel had frozen thicker. How long would it be before the walls and ceiling came together and crushed us?

The air on board was becoming more and more difficult to breathe. Whatever was in the tanks had to be saved for the men working out on the ice. But even that supply would be empty the day after tomorrow!

Hour after hour, we chopped away at the ice. Thirteen feet remained, then ten, then six. But the air reservoirs were now almost empty! The two days were up!

The men on the ship were overcome with a

Chopping Away at the Ice

terrible weariness from the lack of fresh air. Some were unconscious and a few were close to death.

Still three feet of ice remained. The work was going too slowly for us to survive. Then Captain Nemo decided to try crushing the last three feet of ice with the ship itself. Even though he was breathing as little air as we were, he still managed to think, plan and act!

He raised the *Nautilus* off the ice where it had been resting and moved it over above the trench. Water was pumped into the reservoirs to increase the ship's weight.

Slowly the *Nautilus* began to sink. We waited and listened and prayed. I was dizzy from the lack of air, but I soon heard the ice tremble and crack beneath us.

"We're going through!" Conseil murmured in my ear. I was too weak to answer, but I squeezed his hand to let him know I heard.

Dizzy from the Lack of Air

As soon as we were free in the water, the ship started traveling north at a terrifying speed. But how long would it take to reach the other side of the Great Ice Barrier where we could surface? Another day? I would be dead before then!

My face was purple, my lips were blue, and my mind was no longer able to think. I couldn't hear or see anything. As the hours passed, I felt death approaching. . .

"Hold on, Monsieur," whispered Conseil. "We are below an ice field now, and the captain is going to try to break through."

I felt the ship slant upward and heard the roar of its powerful engines. On the first try, the ice cracked a little. We went back down and struck again at full speed. An opening! Finally, with one last effort, we rushed up and broke through to the surface. The hatch sprang open, and pure air came flooding into the *Nautilus*!

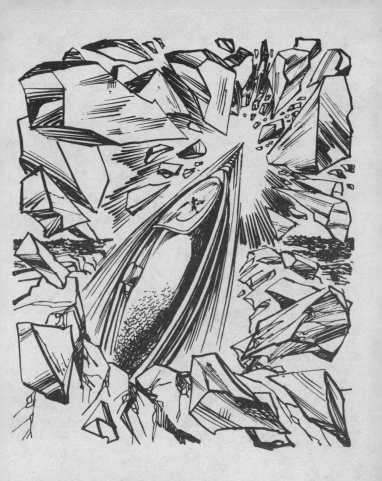

Breaking Through the Ice

Underwater Cliffs of the Bahama Islands

Chapter 16
The Attack of the Squid

Once we were safely in the waters of the Atlantic, everyone seemed to relax. That is, everyone except Captain Nemo. In the month that had passed since our escape from the Great Ice Barrier, he had left me totally alone in my studies and no longer came into the lounge to explain the wonders of the sea.

Towards the end of April, we were cruising below the surface of the Atlantic near the Bahama Islands. Through the windows, I saw the huge underwater cliffs that formed the base of this island group. These cliffs were hollowed out with deep caves where monstrous squid made their homes.

Suddenly, the *Nautilus* stopped. A blow made the ship tremble violently. Ned, Conseil, and I rushed to the window, then froze!

There, before our eyes wriggled a terrible monster—a giant squid twenty-five feet long. The eight long snakelike tentacles coming out of its head were twisting about furiously. Suckers on the inside of each tentacle had fastened themselves to the window.

The monster's mouth—a horny beak—opened and closed rapidly. Its long body, with a bump in the middle, formed a huge fleshy mass which weighed at least 50,000 pounds!

Soon, several other squid appeared and swam all around the *Nautilus*, grinding their beaks against her steel hull.

Just then, Captain Nemo entered the lounge and closed the panels. He looked worried.

"Is something wrong, Captain?" I asked.

The Giant Squid

"Yes, Professor," he said, "one of these squid has his horned beak caught in our propeller and we can't move."

"What can you do?" I asked.

"Surface the ship and wipe them out! But our bullets have no effect on their soft flesh, so we have to fight them hand to hand with axes!"

"And with a harpoon, Captain," added Ned. We left the lounge and joined the crew in the companionway. Captain Nemo gave everyone an axe. Then he popped the hatch.

Within seconds, a long tentacle slid down the opening towards us. Captain Nemo raised his axe and cut the wriggling arm in two.

As we made our way up the ladder, two other tentacles grabbed the sailor in front of the captain and pulled him out. Captain Nemo let out a cry and rushed up the ladder. The poor man was being clutched by the tentacles and waved about in the air. He was

The Squid Captures a Sailor.

choking, but he managed to shout, "Help Help!"

I was stunned to hear these word screamed out in French. So I did have a fel low countryman on board after all! And i his moment of death, he had forgotten th strange speech he had used on board. He ha gasped his dying words in his native lan guage!

But the poor man was done for. Nothin could save him from such a powerful grip Nevertheless, Captain Nemo hurled himsel at the squid and, with repeated blows of hi axe, cut off seven of its tentacles. But just a he rushed at the eighth—the one crushin the sailor—the squid let out a spray of blac ink. We were all blinded by it for severa moments. When the spray cleared, the squi had disappeared, and with it, the unfortunat sailor!

Meanwhile, we were attacking the rest

Captain Nemo Attacks the Squid.

the squid as they climbed up the sides of the ship. We chopped tentacles all around us amid sprays of blood and black ink.

Ned kept plunging his harpoon into the seagreen eyes of these monsters. But suddenly, he was knocked over by a tentacle from behind. The squid's huge mouth opened over Ned and was about to cut him in two when Captain Nemo raced over and buried his axe between the squid's enormous jaws. Ned jumped up and plunged his harpoon deep into the creature's triple heart!

"I owed you this!" Captain Nemo called to Ned. "A squid for a shark!"

Ned bowed his head without answering.

By now, all the wounded or dead squid had disappeared into the sea.

Captain Nemo, covered with ink and blood, stood on the platform looking at the sea which had swallowed up one of his men. Tears ran down his cheeks.

"A Squid for a Shark!"

"What Are You Doing Here?"

Chapter 17
Captain Nemo's Revenge

After the bloody battle with the squid, I came to realize that I could no longer stay on board the *Nautilus*. But I had to try one last time to see if Captain Nemo would let us leave willingly.

I found him in his cabin bent over his work table writing. He frowned as I entered.

"What are you doing here?" he demanded. "I'm busy working."

"Monsieur," I said calmly, "I have to talk to you about something which cannot wait."

"Monsieur Aronnax, what I am doing cannot

wait either! This book I am writing contains all my studies on the sea. With God's help, it will not die with me. The book is signed with my real name and tells the story of my life and work. It will be sealed in a small unsinkable box and will be thrown into the sea by the last man to survive on the *Nautilus* when her end comes."

"Captain, I agree that your studies must not be lost. But who knows where the currents will take the box? Perhaps I could keep this book for you if you gave us our freedom."

"Monsieur Aronnax," cried the captain, "I will say now what I said seven months ago. Whoever enters the *Nautilus* never leaves it! Now get out of here and never speak to me of this again!"

When I reported the captain's words to my two friends, we all agreed that escape was now urgent! We were only a few miles off the coast of New York. What better chance could

"Get Out of Here!"

we hope for!

But just before dark, a hurricane hit New York. Rain was beating down in torrents, and winds were gusting up to 100 miles per hour. It would be suicide to risk an escape in a sea with fifty-foot-high waves!

The storm drove us far out into the North Atlantic. We were all in a state of despair as the *Nautilus* headed east across the ocean.

By June 1, we were three hundred miles from the coast of Ireland, cruising on the surface. I was in the lounge reading when I heard a dull explosion outside the ship.

I rushed up on deck and found Ned and Conseil already there.

"They're firing at us!" cried Ned as he pointed at a ship six miles away. "It looks like a warship, and I hope it comes and sinks this cursed *Nautilus!*"

Just then, another shell hit the water.

"Why are they firing at us?" I cried. "We

"They're Firing at Us!"

didn't attack them fir . . . ." Then suddenly, everything became clear!

Commander Farragut probably had reported to the world that the narwhal was really a submarine. And warships were now searching every ocean for this terrible ship.

I finally had to admit that Captain Nemo was really using the *Nautilus* for revenge! He was attacking the ships of the world regardless of their country. And that night he locked us in the cell and drugged us, it was probably to keep us from seeing an attack! And the sailor now buried in the coral cemetery was probably wounded in a collision!

There was no other explanation. Part of Captain Nemo's mysterious life was becoming clear. But so much was still unexplained!

"Perhaps we can signal them," said Ned. "Then maybe they'll understand we're friends."

He took out his handkerchief to wave in

Commander Farragut's Report

the air. But no sooner had he unfolded it than his arm was struck by a fist of iron.

"You fool!" cried Captain Nemo. "Do you want me to nail you to the spur of the *Nautilus* before we ram that ship? Go below, immediately! All of you!"

"Captain," I protested, "are you really going to attack this ship?"

Captain Nemo's face was twisted with rage as he replied, "Monsieur, I am going to *sink* it! They have attacked me, but my attack will be even more terrible. They shall all die! They are the killers and I am the victim. Because of them, I lost everything I ever loved—my country, my wife, my children, my father, my mother! I saw them all die! Everything I hate is there! Now shut your mouth and go below!"

We raced down to my cabin. Once the door was closed, I gasped, "We must escape! He's gone mad! We must try to warn that ship!"

A Fist of Iron

"Then let us prepare to leave as soon as it is dark!" said Ned.

Night came, but our opportunity to escape did not. Captain Nemo stayed on deck until dawn, when the warship's cannons began firing again.

Then Captain Nemo gave the order to dive. I realized that he was planning to ram the warship from below where it was not protected by heavy steel plates.

"My friends," I said to Ned and Conseil, "this terrible day of June 2 is beginning. May God save us!"

The *Nautilus'* speed increased to the point where its entire hull trembled. Suddenly I felt a blow, then heard the steel spur pushing into something with scraping sounds. The *Nautilus* had gone right through the hull of the warship like a needle going through a piece of cloth!

I couldn't stand it any longer. I rushed into

"Like a Needle Going Through a Cloth"

the lounge, half out of my mind. Captain Nemo was standing there, silently gazing out of the window.

The huge warship was sinking below the surface, and the *Nautilus* was following it down to watch its death struggle. Sailors were climbing up the masts trying to save themselves, but their bodies finally floated free as the sea pulled them down.

I was frozen with horror and unable to catch my breath!

When the ship hit the ocean floor, Captain Nemo turned away. He opened the door to his cabin and went inside.

Through the open door, I saw him go over to a portrait of a young woman and two small children. He gazed at it for several minutes, then clutched it to his chest. With the portrait still in his hands, he sank to his knees and burst into deep sobs!

Captain Nemo's Family

No Idea Where They Are

Chapter 18
Escape!

The *Nautilus* continued on its way as if nothing had happened. But my feelings of horror towards Captain Nemo stayed with me. No matter how much he had suffered at the hands of his fellow men, he had no right to punish them the way he had.

I no longer saw the captain at all. We stayed underwater for the next twenty days, surfacing only to renew our air supply. Our position was no longer marked on the map, so I had no idea where we were.

One morning, I awoke to find Ned leaning

over me. In a low voice, he said, "Our chance has come! I went up on deck when we surfaced and made out some land about twenty miles to the east. Meet us at the dinghy at ten tonight!"

"I'll be there, Ned," I replied.

The rest of that day seemed to last forever. I didn't dare leave my cabin for fear of meeting Captain Nemo and having him see the horror I felt for him.

But at seven o'clock, I went to the lounge to take one last look at the wonders of nature and art collected there. I felt a stab of regret that these treasures would one day be destroyed at the bottom of the sea along with the man who had gathered them.

Then I returned to my cabin and dressed in my thick sea clothes. I gathered up my notes and tucked them carefully inside my jacket. My heart was beating fast, and I was unable to control my nerves.

One Last Look

I tried to stretch out on my bed and relax. All the events of the past ten months on board the *Nautilus* passed before my eyes: the disappearance of the *Abraham Lincoln,* the underwater hunting expeditions, running aground at Torres Strait, the attack by the cannibals of New Guinea, the coral cemetery, the tunnel beneath Suez, the diver and the gold bars at Crete, the treasure at Vigo Bay, the lost continent of Atlantis, the Great Ice Barrier, the South Pole, the digging out of the ice tunnel, the fight with the squid, and the attack on the warship, watching it sink with all hands. . .

Before I knew it, it was almost ten o'clock. I opened my door and crept down the gangway towards the lounge. Soft, sad music was coming from the organ. Captain Nemo was in there and I had to pass him to get out!

I crept across the darkened room without being noticed. Just as I reached the door to

Remembering. . .

the library, Captain Nemo struck one resounding chord on the organ and cried out in the darkness the last words I ever heard from him. "Almighty God! Enough! Enough!"

Was he finally regretting. . .? I didn't have time to think now. I rushed through the library, into the companionway, and up into the dinghy.

Ned and Conseil bolted the hatches behind me. Then, just as Ned started to loosen the bolts holding the dinghy to the submarine, we heard voices talking excitedly inside the *Nautilus.*

Had someone discovered our escape? Were they looking for us?. . .No! One word that the crew kept repeating over and over told me what was causing all the excitement.

"The Maelstrom! The Maelstrom!"

The Maelstrom! Could a more frightening word reach the ears of any sailor? The Maelstrom, off the coast of Norway, was the

"Almighty God! Enough! Enough!"

most violent whirlpool in the world! No ship had ever escaped its raging current! Was the *Nautilus* about to be dragged down into its depths just as we were escaping?

Had the *Nautilus* been caught up in the Maelstrom by accident? Or was this some plan of Captain Nemo's?...I had no more time to think. The *Nautilus* started spinning around and around in smaller and smaller circles. And the dinghy, still attached to her hull, was carried along with her at an incredible speed. We were terrified! Our blood stopped circulating! Our nerves were numb! We were at death's door!

"We have to screw the bolts back down," gasped Ned. "It's our only chance...."

But before he could finish, we heard a loud crack. The bolts had broken! The dinghy was torn from the ship and thrown into the middle of the whirlpool like a stone hurled from a slingshot!

Caught in the Maelstrom!

My head hit the side of the iron dinghy and I lost consciousness.

What happened that night, how we escaped the whirlpool and survived, neither Ned, nor Conseil, nor I can ever say.

When I came to, I was lying in a fisherman's cottage on one of the islands off the coast of Norway. My two friends tearfully embraced me the moment I opened my eyes.

Thus ended the voyage which took us 60,000 miles, or 20,000 leagues, under the sea. Will people believe me?. . .I do not know. But for ten months, I had traveled under the oceans of the world and gazed at their many wonders.

What became of the *Nautilus*? Did it escape the Maelstrom? Is Captain Nemo still alive? If so, has he finished with his terrible revenge? Will the seas one day wash up the book containing his life story? Will I ever find out his real name?

Saved!

I hope so. I also hope that the *Nautilus* survived in that terrible whirlpool where so many other ships were wrecked.

If it has, and if Captain Nemo still lives in the ocean, then I hope with all my heart that his hatred for the world has come to an end. I hope that he is peacefully exploring the seas and will one day share his vast scientific knowledge with the whole human race!

Does Captain Nemo Still Live?

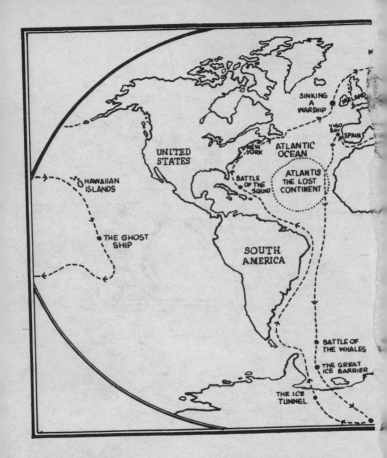

The 20,000-League

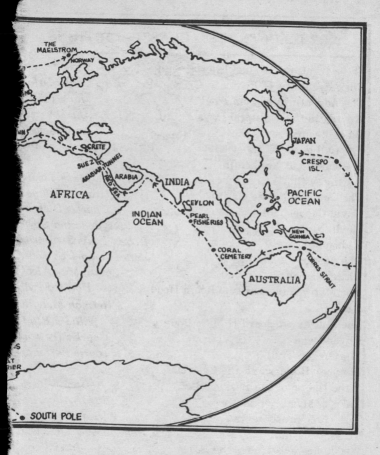

THE
MAELSTROM
● NORWAY

● JAPAN

CRESPO
ISL. ●

PACIFIC
OCEAN

AFRICA

● CRETE
SUEZ
ARABIAN TUNNEL
RED SEA
ARABIA

INDIA

CEYLON
PEARL
FISHERIES

NEW
GUINEA

INDIAN
OCEAN

CORAL
CEMETERY

TORRES STRAIT

AUSTRALIA

S
AT
RIER

● SOUTH POLE

Trip of the *Nautilus*

ILLUSTRATED CLASSIC EDITIONS

MOBY BOOKS